A TALE WHOSE TIME HAS COME

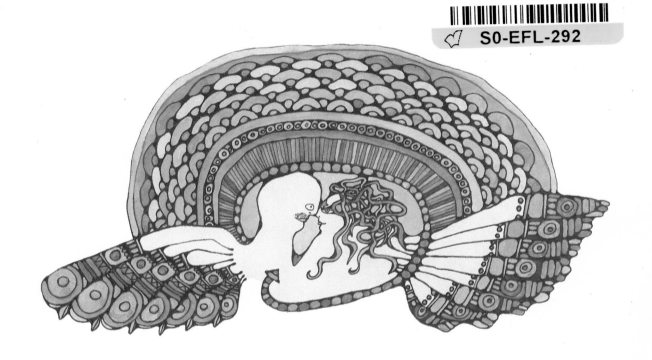

Tale by Robert Siegel
Pictures by Karol Barske

Hidden House/Flash Books
palo alto, ca. new york

For Howie, Nancy & Nunzio

Hidden House/Flash Books
A Division of Music Sales Corporation

Hidden House Publications © 1975

All Rights Reserved
Printed in United States of America
ISBN 08256-3807-0

Distribution:
Quick Fox Inc.
33 West 60th Street
New York, N.Y. 10023

Yoj was a man ahead of his time

Which is another way of saying: He was growing old very quickly

1

Treah was a woman waiting for something perfect.

Which is another way of saying she was ahead of her time.

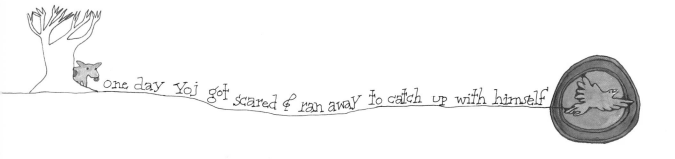

one day Yoj got scared & ran away to catch up with himself

on that very day Treah also ran away—She was tired of waiting

The next moment,
Yoj met Treah
in a subway station next to the gumball machine

Yoj said,
"Do we have to be adults?"

"Certainly not"
said Treah

They kissed &
laughed &
hugged
& stole the gumball machine
& they ran home
(which was wherever they were)
kissing & hugging & laughing & blowing bubbles

5

That night, Treah & Yoj
lay in their yard
which was next to their home (which was wherever they were)
& watched the world floating by

6

7

They began to cry for the moon:
"You never get to meet the sun,"
They whined

& they cried for the stars:
"If only you could see the blue sky"

& they cried for the night:
"You never see the day--
You're never all together"

Just then, a dog came by.

10

11

"Whattaya want?"
  asked Yoj & Treah as they cried.

"It'scoolit'scoolit'scool
  It'scoolit'scoolit'scool"
said the dog.

"Whattaya mean?"
  They said as they stopped crying.

"The trees, the trees,
  they know it all--they see them both
  they bring it all
together."

"But so do we"
  said Yoj & Treah.

"That's right" said the dog.
"We bring it all together--
  It'scoolit'scoolit'scool"

Yoj & Treah laughed--
  The dog was right.
"Say, what's your name, anyway?"
  They asked.

"Nunzio, Nunzio —
  & it'scoolit'scoolit'scoolit'scool"

13

So Nunzio, Yoj & Treah
lay amongst the trees &
their dreams danced through the night
like a cat
nuzzling against a hand
for warmth

The dance told them all
told them all

For what is a dream
but a poem
not yet born

14

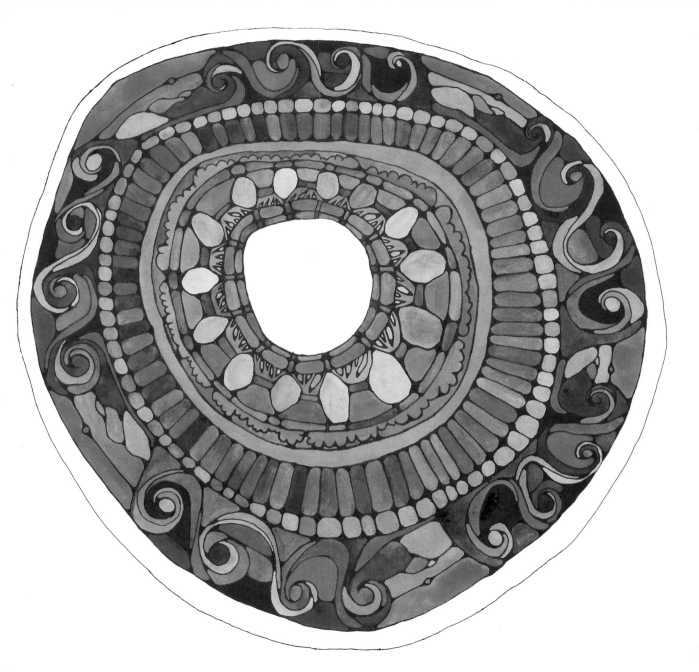

15

In the morning
Yoj wrote his
first prayer

Yoj's Prayer:

On the seventh day
God ended his work
Which he had made
& laughed at himself

16

17

18

Treah also
wrote a prayer :

Something now
is
Something perfect

19

Nunzio sang his prayer
to the neighbors--

Nunzio's prayer:

Who Cares?

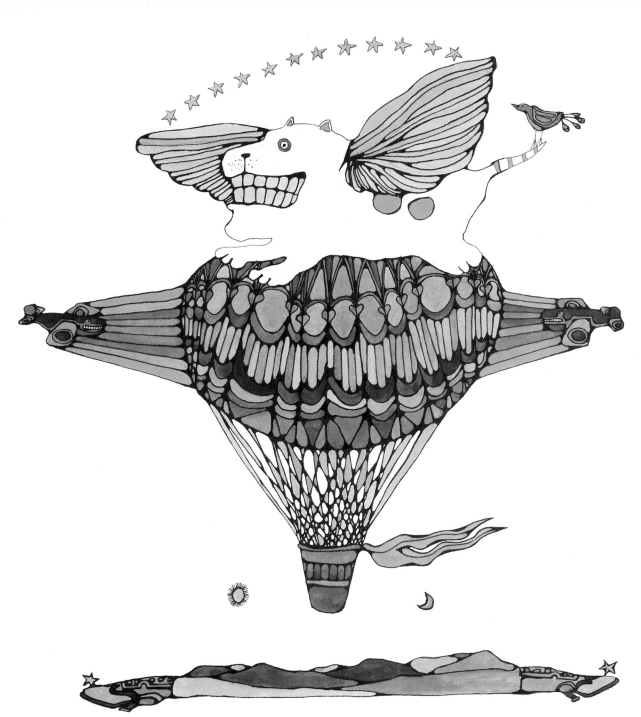

21

For days & moments
they sang songs
listened to the music
watched the Lone Ranger
& gave each other all the secrets of their love

A new world born
was a new world shared

23

24

Yoj became an Umpire
he would put on his mask
stand in front of the mirror
& laugh till his sides hurt

"You're OUT"
he would scream ferociously

"You're SAFE"
he would bellow with
the fervor of a preacher

25

& oh, how he loved to
get on the subway,
go downtown
& call the GAME

26

27

"You're OUT!"
he declared to the fashion models
in the department store
windows

"You're SAFE"
he purred into the ear
of the Pigeon Lady

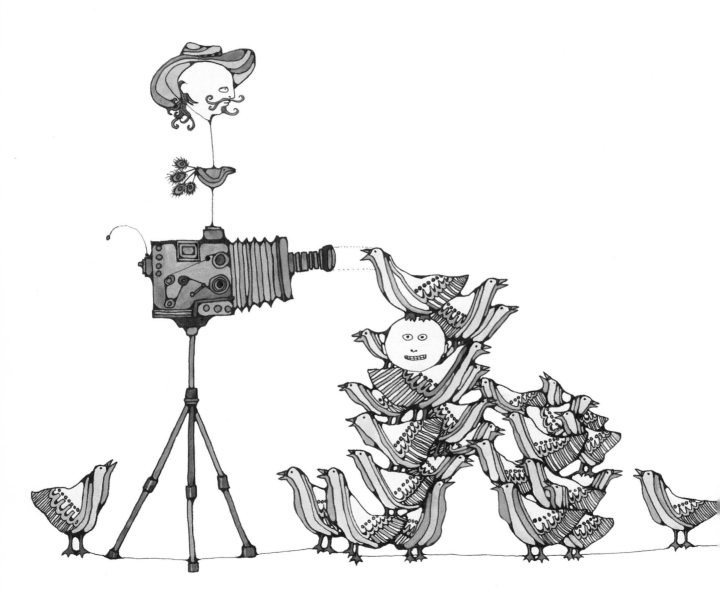

30

"You're OUT," he said,
mimicking the man with the
camera

"You're SAFE," he said,
putting his arm around
the Duck Man

32

Treah drew things:
She drew matchbooks & chimneys &
bicycles
& shoes

33

"Why don't you ever draw me?"
Nunzio would ask
"Or Yoj
or the trees in the yard?"

Treah said No.

"Flowers & trees & animals
& people
are not for drawing
they are for
being with"

35

36

Nunzio decided to change the world.
"I'm gonna organize
the Time Ladies"

"Who?" asked Treah

"You know, the ladies
who tell you the time
on the telephone"

"But what will you organize them for"
asked Yoj

"Better conditions" said Nunzio, smiling

"Like what?" Yoj & Treah asked

Nunzio said nothing.

Next week, Yoj & Treah
called Time
To see how Nunzio was doing.

"At the time
The time
will be
seven-thirty-four
& ten seconds...

Who cares ??
it's cool it's cool it's cool"

39

One night while
they were all busy
doing nothing 'cept enjoying themselves
they heard this Booming Noise --
shook everything--
Everything

"Someone's at the door" said Nunzio

"Friends!!" screamed Yoj with delight

"Friends!!" echoed Treah, grabbing
                    some pots & pans

They hurried downstairs clanking their pots & pans
          singing the song they made for
                              Friends:
                    VISITOR'S SONG
                         "Hello
                    How are you
              we're glad that you're here
              Come in, be at ease
                    There's nothing to fear
        There are no guests, there are no hosts
          Strangers are friends when you get
                              Close"

                    They opened the door
          & there stood a young looking man
                    with this big white
          sack slung over his shoulder

42

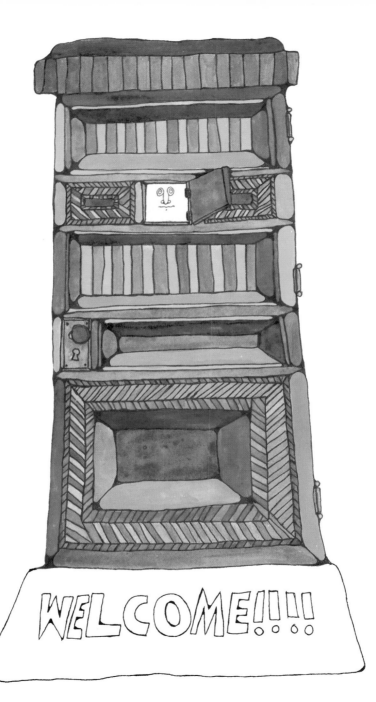

44

"My name is Worrommot"
(He said, stepping inside)
& I'm trying to get home
(Which was wherever he wasn't)
"I need food & a place to sleep"

After he had eaten,
Worrommot looked up at his hosts
& asked
"What do you do?"

"Whattaya mean?"
asked Nunzio

"Don't you do something
with your time?"
said Worrommot

45

"Oh, that"
said Yoj, smiling.
"We feel good--
That's what we do with
our time"
said Treah

"But you must be doing
something ELSE"
declared Worrommot

"I'm changing the world"
said Nunzio
"& I'm an Umpire"
said Yoj
"& I draw things"
said Treah

46

47

'Aah, you're an ARTIST,"
Worrommot said to Treah.

"No, I just draw things,"
Treah said to Worrommot.

49

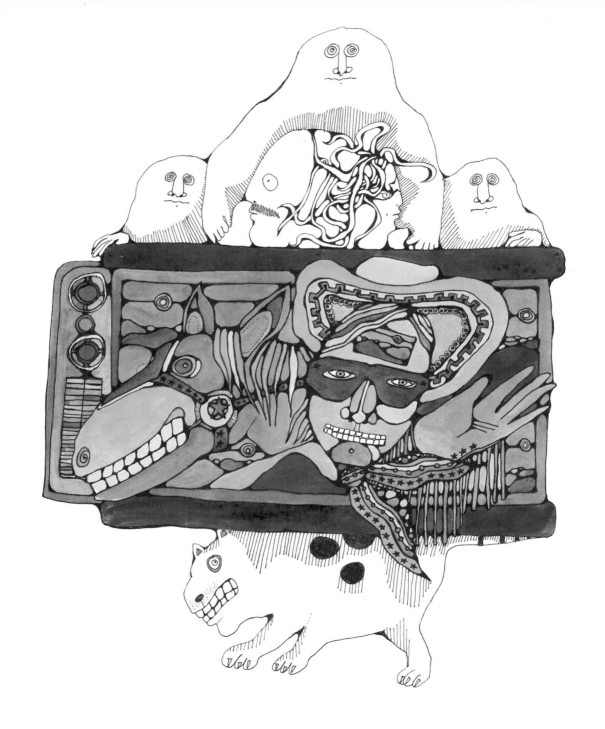

50

"& we dance & sing
& listen to the music
& watch the Lone Ranger"
said Nunzio

"But what do you do with your Life?"
Worrommot was getting upset

Nunzio, Yoj & Treah were confused.
"Whattaya mean?"
They asked

51

"Well, take me"
he began. "I play the flute
& the piano
& I write.
Someday I'm going to be a great
Musician
or a great
Writer"

"Does it feel good to play
Music?"
asked Treah

"Of course"
said Worrommot
"It feels great
to know that someday
I might
BE GREAT!!"

Yoj & Treah & Nunzio
were even more confused

"Does it feel good
just to play?"
asked Yoj

53

Now Worrommot was confused.
"Haven't you ever felt
that someday you might
BE GREAT!!"
he cried out

54

WORROMMOT
★ A GREAT ★
MAN
★

55

56

"Who Cares" said Nunzio,
starting to clank on the pots & pans

"Hey! The Lone Ranger is on!"
shouted Treah

Yoi put his arm around Worrommot
"Would you like to try on my Umpire's mask?"

In an instant they had formed
a circle around Worrommot
& danced him to the Lone Ranger
What could he do but laugh?

For almost a week
they danced & sang as never before;
They even made a new song
NEW SONG:
"There is no beginning
There is no end
Today is a moment
forever, forever
A home for the
Free"

Worrommot was learning to play

57

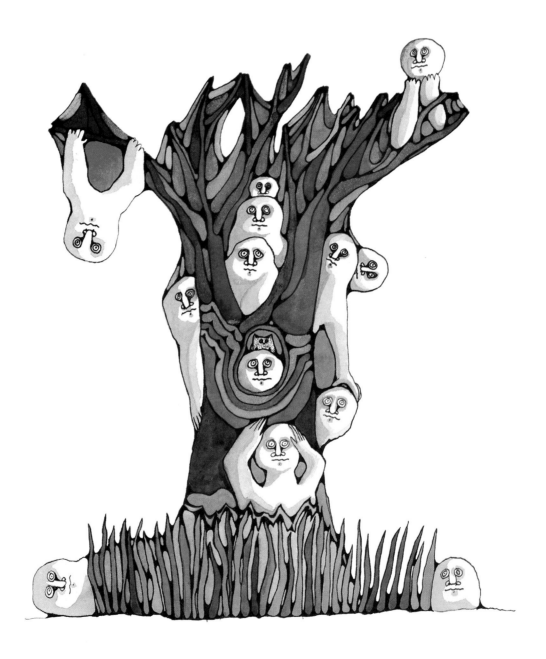

But at night, Worromma
would go off to the yard
& he would try to sleep
He'd move from
side to side
roll & tumble & toss & turn & jump up & down
No Sleep.

59

60

& Then the Black Mist
 would come, settling all around
 pinning him to the ground

"What do you want?"
 he cried out with fear

& The Mist spoke with a scolding anger:
"When did you last pick up your flute?
 When did you last play your piano?
 When did you last write me a story?"

"Go way, go way
 Please go away"

"Come home, come home
 it is time to
 Come home
 Come back at once
 & I'll leave you
 Alone"

On the seventh morning
Worrommot decided to leave
he wrote a note

Worrommot's note:

Thanks for a nice time
but I must find my home
Piddling & Fiddling
Dillying & Dallying
it's just not for me
I gotta create--
who knows
someday I might
be great

Then he began to pack
furiously throwing everythi
into his sack
while the voice of the night
climbed up his back
saying
"hurry-hurry-hurry

All of a sudden he jumped bac
Nunzio was standing right in front of h
smiling
Nunzio took a long stretch & said
as he yawned
"You know,
you already are great"
Worrommot grabbed his sack
& quickly walked past Nunzio
into the kitchen

62

63

64

Treah was sitting
at the table
sipping some coffee.
The birds in the yard
were singing,
the kitchen was very still,
Worrommot rinsed a cup
& poured some coffee.

He looked at Treah

Then he went to the cabinet
to get some sugar --

He looked at Treah
he felt like he was
making a lot of noise.

He was gonna make himself
a sandwitch
but when
he opened the breadbox
there was this sign
on top of the bread
which said:

You know,
you already are great
love,
Treah

65

Worrommot dropped his coffee
grabbed his sack
& walked even faster
past Treah, then Nunzio
almost running right out the front door
where he ran smack into Yoj

Yoj went down
Worrommot went down
groceries went flying

After a minute or so
they both sat up, looking right at each other
The first laugh sounded
like they were wheezing through their noses
Then it turned into big, open mouthed moose calls
& pretty soon they were both lying
flat on their backs
rolling around
letting go
high
high pitched
monkey
ooogles

Right when the ooogles got their second wind
Yoj shouted---
"Hey, you know what?"
"What?"
gulped Worrommot between ooogles
"You already are great !!"
screamed Yoj, ooogling even harder
"I'm already great !!"
screamed Worrommot ooogling
so hard he was holding his stomach
"Yeah!!!"
ooogleooogled Yoj
"Yeah!!!"
ooogleooogled Worrommot

& there they were, rolling around
ooogling & ooogling
holding their stomachs
ooogling & ooogling,
for who knows how long
(Who can measure the length of the
great ooogle Ooogle)

67

Worrommot stayed
for quite a while
watching the Lone Ranger
& listening to the music
& writing his stories
& playing his flute
& hardly ever being
bothered by the Black Mist

& he would get up
in the morning
mingle with the sun
sway with the leaves
in time to the breeze
& sing
his
morning song

Morning Song:

There is no beginning
There is no end
Today is a moment
forever, forever
a home for the Free
it's good to create
it's good to just be.

69

About Robert and Karol

Robert met Karol's other-self illuminating a gallery wall at the University of Illinois. That caused him to seek her out in person.

This book was created as the two of them traveled from Chicago to San Francisco, via Mexico, in a 1964 Econoline Van named Sugaree.

Karol is now living in San Franciso where she's involved in painting, loving and cleaning out the Purple Heart Thrift Store.

Robert is seriously involved in writing stories as well as writing and playing music. Robert is also a college dropout in dedicated pursuit of the perfectly thin stone that will do at least ten skips across any body of water.

And yes, Nunzio really does exist.